Acting Edition

CW00549671

JOB

by Max Wolf Friedlich

Copyright © 2024 by Max Wolf Friedlich
All Rights Reserved

JOB is fully protected under the copyright laws of the United States of America, the British Commonwealth, including Canada, and all member countries of the Berne Convention for the Protection of Literary and Artistic Works, the Universal Copyright Convention, and/or the World Trade Organization conforming to the Agreement on Trade Related Aspects of Intellectual Property Rights. All rights, including professional and amateur stage productions, recitation, lecturing, public reading, motion picture, radio broadcasting, television, online/digital production, and the rights of translation into foreign languages are strictly reserved.

ISBN 978-0-573-71105-3

www.concordtheatricals.com
www.concordtheatricals.co.uk

FOR PRODUCTION INQUIRIES

UNITED STATES AND CANADA
info@concordtheatricals.com
1-866-979-0447

UNITED KINGDOM AND EUROPE
licensing@concordtheatricals.co.uk
020-7054-7298

Each title is subject to availability from Concord Theatricals Corp., depending upon country of performance. Please be aware that *JOB* may not be licensed by Concord Theatricals Corp. in your territory. Professional and amateur producers should contact the nearest Concord Theatricals Corp. office or licensing partner to verify availability.

CAUTION: Professional and amateur producers are hereby warned that *JOB* is subject to a licensing fee. The purchase, renting, lending or use of this book does not constitute a license to perform this title(s), which license must be obtained from Concord Theatricals Corp. prior to any performance. Performance of this title(s) without a license is a violation of federal law and may subject the producer and/or presenter of such performances to civil penalties. Both amateurs and professionals considering a production are strongly advised to apply to the appropriate agent before starting rehearsals, advertising, or booking a theatre. A licensing fee must be paid whether the title(s) is presented for charity or gain and whether or not admission is charged. Professional/Stock licensing fees are quoted upon application to Concord Theatricals Corp.

This work is published by Samuel French, an imprint of Concord Theatricals Corp.

No one shall make any changes in this title(s) for the purpose of production. No part of this book may be reproduced, stored in a retrieval system, scanned, uploaded, or transmitted in any form, by any means, now known or yet to be invented, including mechanical, electronic, digital, photocopying, recording, videotaping, or otherwise, without the prior written permission of the publisher. No one shall share this title(s), or any part of this title(s), through any social media or file hosting websites.

For all inquiries regarding motion picture, television, online/digital and other media rights, please contact Concord Theatricals Corp.

MUSIC AND THIRD-PARTY MATERIALS USE NOTE

Licensees are solely responsible for obtaining formal written permission from copyright owners to use copyrighted music and/or other copyrighted third-party materials (e.g. artworks, logos) in the performance of this play and are strongly cautioned to do so. If no such permission is obtained by the licensee, then the licensee must use only original music and materials that the licensee owns and controls. Licensees are solely responsible and liable for clearances of all third-party copyrighted materials, including without limitation music, and shall indemnify the copyright owners of the play(s) and their licensing agent, Concord Theatricals Corp., against any costs, expenses, losses and liabilities arising from the use of such copyrighted third-party materials by licensees. For music, please contact the appropriate music licensing authority in your territory for the rights to any incidental music.

IMPORTANT BILLING AND CREDIT REQUIREMENTS

If you have obtained performance rights to this title, please refer to your licensing agreement for important billing and credit requirements.

JOB began previews at The SoHo Playhouse on September 6, 2023. It was produced by Hannah Getts, Russell Kahn, and Danielle Perelman. It was directed by Michael Herwitz, with dramaturgy by Hannah Getts, set design by Scott Penner, costume design by Michelle J. Li, lighting design by Mextly Couzin, and sound design by Jessie Char and Maxwell Neely-Cohen. The production featured photography/creative direction by Josh Aronson, graphic design by Julian Alicea a.k.a. The BRAIN-WAVE, music by Cautious Clay, and merchandise by JUJU Merk & Ben Gabriel of donothing.nyc. The production stage managers were Chris Steckel and Rachel A. Zucker. The cast was as follows:

JANE . . . . Sydney Lemmon
LOYD . . . . .Peter Friedman

JOB transferred to The Connelly Theater on January 19, 2024. The production was produced by Hannah Getts and Alex Levy. The creative team remained the same with the following additions: associate costume designer Lily Cunicelli, mask designer Patrice Escandon, associate sound designer Julian Evans, sub stage manager Liv Gunderson, associate director Jessie Klueter, and production manager Chris Luner. The cast was the same with the following additions:

JANE UNDERSTUDY . . . . .Arianna Gayle Stucki
LOYD UNDERSTUDY . . . . Mark Zeisler

JOB was originally written in the IAMA Theatre Company's 2019–2020 Under 30 Playwrights Lab (Stefanie Black, Artistic Director).

CHARACTERS

JANE – female, twenty-five to thirty, white, young professional living in the Bay Area, knows how to dress to fit in, "self-aware" to a fault, wouldn't be out of place at SoulCycle.

LOYD – male, sixties or older, white, lived in the East Bay his whole life, rocks a hippie-adjacent sort of look, has a high opinion of himself, wouldn't be out of place at a Grateful Dead show.

SETTING

Downtown San Francisco

TIME

January, 2020

AUTHOR'S NOTES

Style notes

[ ] indicates a word that is implied but not said

/ indicates where the next speaker should interrupt the current speaker

A … between lines of dialogue is a beat where the speaker holds the energy/focus during the pause.

Production notes

When Jane puts something in " " she is expressing disdain for that thing.

This is a period piece.

The room should feel real because it is. Resist the urge to set the play anywhere "metaphorical" or like…"liminal."

In that same vein, the things that aren't really happening…aren't really happening.

The more…"out there" sounds should happen with lights – we are going somewhere else for a moment.

Music before and after the play is important.

Watch *We're All Going to The World's Fair* (2021, dir. Jane Schoenbrun), read *Uncanny Valley* by Anna Wiener.

ACKNOWLEDGMENTS

Thank you to the 2019–2020 IAMA Theatre Under 30 Lab who read the earliest drafts of this play and offered invaluable feedback, support, and friendship – Laura Donney, Ken Greller, Madeline Hendricks Lewen, Nicholas Pilapal, and Adriana Santos.

Thank you to the actors who helped this play take shape – Emily James, Tom Amendes, Tim Barker, Delia Cunningham, Arliss Howard, and my cherished little brother/son Alex O'Shea.

Thank you to Samuel Dallas, Nathan Gehen, Devin Ramirez, and everyone at Showtown.

Thank you to Jim Byk, Louisa Pancoast, and everyone at The Press Room.

Thank you to Joe Meyer for going above and beyond for this play every single day, every single night.

Thank you Cody Victor and Jarrett Jung for making TikToks with me to try to get us popping.

Thank you to Connor Boyd, an internet stranger turned friend who posted the TikTok about this show that changed my life. I guess sort of thank you TikTok also? I dunno.

Thank you to all the bosses who fired me. It means the world.

Thank you to Rachel Viola for taking a chance on an eighteen-year-old playwright however many years ago.

Thank you Michael Fields for your mentorship and guidance.

Thank you to my community at the Wayfinder Experience for teaching me to be brave.

Thank you to Mary Woodbine for teaching me how to love unconditionally.

Thank you Peter and Sydney. It has been the honor of my life to watch you perform this play.

Thank you to Michael Herwitz for pushing me to be a better collaborator and friend. You inspire me as a theater maker, but you inspire me even more as a human being. I love you. How cool is this, dude??? They published the play! I can't wait for the next one. Me and you, pal. Me and you.

Thank you to my friends. I am only ever trying to make you guys laugh and proud and that's honestly my like…"artist statement." I hope you feel as supported by me as I do by you.

To my friend Jesse Galganov – זיכרונו לברכה

Thank you to Jim Friedlich for being my role model. Thank you for always picking up the phone.

And above all thank you to Melissa Stern – my favorite artist in any medium, always and forever.

If anyone is curious where this play comes from go to www.melissa-stern.com

To Hannah
This play is not "for" you – it is because of you.

(January 2020.)

(This year's gonna be the one – it's gonna be sooo sick. New Year's resolutions are still within reach; the election will surely change everything for the better.)

(Downtown San Francisco.)

(A therapist's office – a couch, IKEA lamps, some ferns. The Bay Bridge can be seen from the window, lines of cars clogging the road in both directions.)

(There's a desktop computer, filing drawers, some snacks [Kirkland cashews, Luna Bars],* a box of tissues. On the walls, some vaguely South Asian art purchased on a road trip through New Mexico.)

(Lights up.)

*(**JANE** holds a gun to **LOYD**'s head. She carries a cloth tote bag. **LOYD** holds a pen and legal pad. She's shaking – too much adrenaline to cry, in over her head.)*

LOYD. *(Steady.)* Why / don't you –

JANE. Don't say anything just –

LOYD. My name is –

JANE. I KNOW WHO YOU ARE JUST – DON'T TALK. PLEASE.

---

* A license to produce *JOB* does not include a license to publicly display any branded logos or trademarked images. Licensees must acquire rights for any logos and/or images or create their own.

(She shoots – click.)

(Reset – almost like blinking.)

*(**JANE** holds a gun to **LOYD**'s head. He looks her deep in the eye. He smirks.)*

LOYD. You did it.

You were right about everything.

(He screams – a super villain. He lunges at her.)

(She shoots. Click. Reset.)

*(**JANE**'s not holding the gun – she's calm, pedestrian. **LOYD** smiles at her.)*

– no no no don't even mention it – happy to squeeze you in. In general, do Wednesdays at this time work? Remind me also to give you a parking pass if you – did you say you drove?

(Click. Reset.)

*(**JANE** holds a gun to **LOYD**'s head. There's something somber about her this time – vacant.)*

Hang on, hang on now –

(She puts the gun to her own head.)

Wait wait just please – WAIT!

(Click. Reset.)

*(**JANE** holds a gun to **LOYD**'s head.)*

– and whatever is happening in your life I promise we can talk about it, I will listen.

(**JANE** *scrutinizes* **LOYD**'s *face, searching for something.* **LOYD** *silently pleads with her. Beat.* **JANE** *finds a shred of doubt. She lowers the gun...slightly... "coming to her senses.")*

JANE. I got confused, I got uhm... I'm so sorry.

LOYD. That's alright –

JANE. No like I am so fucking sorry, holy shit.

(**LOYD** *is not sure what to say.*)

(Terrified.) This is not who I am, I would never like – FUCK!

Are you going to call the police?!

LOYD. I think we can find our breath –

JANE. Can I have some water?

LOYD. Yes, yes absolutely – the water cooler is out in the hall.

(Takes a step towards the door.)

I'll be right back, alright?

JANE. *(Steps in his way, barely thinking.)* I... OK.

LOYD. I'll grab you that water if – would you or – *could I...* should we put the gun in my desk –

JANE. *(Fire alarm.)* NO – I... sorry, I'm good.

(Beat.)

LOYD. You do or *do not* want water?

JANE. I'm good, yeah.

LOYD. Ah OK well if you change your mind, water thingamajig's just out in the hall, the water uh – the water COOLER – just out in the hall there.

...

LOYD. I'm a big believer in water – lot of problems all of us have come down to water and sleep. Man oh man they don't always solve the problem but boy they sure do help.

JANE. ...can we keep going?

LOYD. Keep going...? With –

JANE. Or maybe we can't, maybe I'm just fucked because like – no because like shouldn't you have to tell someone? Like by law, aren't you obligated to...[tell someone.]

LOYD. You're asking if legally I'm required to –

JANE. I don't want you to get in trouble if there's a law where – AND also if I'm gonna get arrested for being a fucking PSYCHO I'd like to just have that HAPPEN and / not wait –

LOYD. *(Gently putting a hand up.)* Let's just – let's talk it through.

In the 60s – or maybe the early 70s – just over the bridge, a Berkeley student stabbed his girlfriend. Fatally, he stabbed her. And prior to doing so he had expressed to his therapist that he was *planning* to kill this young woman – his crime was pre-meditated, he expressed prior intent. And so after their daughter was killed, the girlfriend's family filed a lawsuit that then traveled all the way up to the California Supreme Court where it was determined that it was this guy's *therapist* who was at fault for not sounding the alarm.

"The protective privilege ends where the public peril begins."

And so – and I'm working this through in real time, forgive me – but I suppose the question I should ask you is –

JANE. What happened to the guy?

LOYD. Well yes the doctor at the center of it / all, he –

JANE. The stabber, the guy who stabbed his girlfriend.

LOYD. He was an Indian guy and I believe they released him on the condition he go back to India. Poddar – that was his last name.

...

And for me what's so fascinating is this guy Poddar was what's called an "Untouchable." They're the lowest in the caste system –

JANE. Right that's the...right, that's the like social pyramid in India...?

LOYD. Exactly. The Untouchables deal with waste – be it litter or feces – that's their lot in life, their "role" in society. They're born into it and it's damn near impossible to move up. And so apparently this guy Poddar was one of the *only* people *ever* to go from being in the Untouchable caste to studying at an American university. So just zooming out on that, you've got this one in a billion guy, who makes it all the way to Berkeley, against impossible odds – after all that struggle he goes and does something so horrible that he changes the nature of doctor–patient confidentiality in America forever, I mean ho-ly cow.

...

Do you feel like hurting people?

JANE. *(Less sure.)* No.

LOYD. Do you feel like hurting yourself?

JANE. *(More sure.)* No.

LOYD. That's wonderful, I'm very glad you – and so I think for today the uhm – a boundary.

A boundary for me, that I'd maybe like to set...how would you feel about putting the gun back in your bag?

JANE. Yeah of course I – of course.

> *(Gently places the gun in her bag.)*

I don't think you'll try to escape.

> *(Beat.)*

LOYD. Iiiii can't quite read your tone, / are you –

JANE. Bad joke or...attempt at –

LOYD. *(Forcing a laugh.)* No no that's good, that's – and so how would you feel about if we walked downstairs, chatted alfresco – there's a great little park across the – no?

> *(**JANE** looks confused.)*

(Slowly standing.) In that case what I'm going to do is I'm just going to step out and –

> *(**JANE** flings herself in front of the door. She's embarrassed to be doing so – more of a plea than a threat, begging masquerading as demanding.)*

JANE. I can't imagine how scary that was for you – it was scary for me too – but I promise, I swear like... I will do whatever you need me to do just... I can't be outside right now, I – I haven't slept in a couple days, I haven't – I can't be outside, I just need to get back to work.

LOYD. *(Uncomfortable.)* I hear you.

> *(Beat. Neither knows exactly what to do.)*

I'm told you've seen a few folks in the past – therapy-wise I mean.

JANE. My parents started sending me when I was nine... / uhm...

LOYD. Did you find working with those folks to be fruitful?

JANE. Sorry – that's in my like…"file"?

That I was in therapy like…as a child?

LOYD. Chelsea – your HR person – she gave some very very basic background.

JANE. What else did she tell you about me?

LOYD. Just the basics.

JANE. Just the basics, OK…yeah…great, that's – yeah… awesome.

LOYD. If I can ask –

JANE. I'm an open book – completely open – ask me whatever.

LOYD. How long have you had the gun for?

Or any gun for that matter –

JANE. No no I'm not like a "gun person" –

LOYD. Yes of course not – I didn't mean to sound / accusatory –

JANE. Yeah I've only ever had the one.

LOYD. Just so you're aware – there's no right or wrong answers –

JANE. No totally – I've had it a few months? It's January so yeah – a few months.

LOYD. So the gun is in your bag, you put it away…how do you feel?

JANE. Fucking embarrassed like…shame.

Which is like…useless.

LOYD. Shame can be constructive.

JANE. Sure maybe if you're like…Christian.

LOYD. I'm not an especially spiritual person – at least not in the traditional sense – but I will contend that the people who wrote the Bible down were some very *very* clever people.

We're told that Adam and Eve eat the sort of magical wisdom apple, right?

They eat the apple, realize they're naked, and then... they feel shame.

So *shame* is the very first *feeling* mentioned in the Bible – *wisdom* and *shame* are connected.

JANE. Cool well uh... I don't really feel wiser post like... almost committing murder.

LOYD. Well...next time maybe better for everyone if the gun could stay at home.

JANE. Yes great – I'll try to be less armed "next time."

LOYD. *(Forcing a smile.)* Do you often use humor to help process more serious things?

JANE. No. I'm more of Xanax girlie.

LOYD. Case in point, there it is – the humor.

Are you...interested in discussing medication for anxiety?

I'm a therapist, not a psychiatrist but...

JANE. I'm actually pretty set on the Xanax front.

LOYD. You're prescribed Xanax? I must have missed that on the little one-sheeter they –

JANE. There's a guy in my neighborhood.

He gets them in Mexico, it's over the counter there apparently.

LOYD. And so how often do you take them?

JANE. Just when things feel out of control.

LOYD. Out of control in what sense?

JANE. Out of control – where everything's happening at the same time.

Where you're *here* but you're remembering and figuring out what to do next all at once.

(**LOYD** *nods, clearly confused.*)

Sorry... I just hate talking about myself – it never seems to get me anywhere.

LOYD. Get you anywhere in terms of...?

JANE. When I talk... I don't know, people assume I'm this confident put-together person. But being able to articulate what I'm going through doesn't make it any easier.

LOYD. We can sit here in silence if you want.

JANE. Don't think that's a good use of company money...

LOYD. They have plenty.

JANE. I just don't really want to do this.

LOYD. This meaning...?

JANE. I'm sorry, I shouldn't have said that.

LOYD. No no, don't worry – there's no right or wrong.

JANE. I don't need to be in therapy.

LOYD. Let's maybe...explore that because...to *me* –

JANE. I *WILL* do it – I'll give you whatever you need from me, but like I don't need this as a person like – sorry – I'm being too honest –

LOYD. No such thing.

JANE. I just didn't come here of my own like free will exactly.

LOYD. Wellll you didn't uhm...you didn't exactly want us to leave either so –

JANE. I'm here because of my job.

I'm required to be here – they told me if I want to go back I had to come see you.

LOYD. But so in that way perhaps it's not a requirement.

Maybe you only need to be here if you're determined to go back to the office –

JANE. I have work to do, it's not a choice.

LOYD. You're aware of this I hope but it bears repeating – I don't work / for them –

JANE. But you get to decide if I'm allowed to return to work.

LOYD. I don't know that I'll be *the* deciding factor –

JANE. They probably wish they could just fire me but that could be a lawsuit.

They need an outside doctor to make the final call.

LOYD. I know they have their own internal process as well –

JANE. Trust me I understand their process.

LOYD. Well I'm sure they will take your enthusiasm into consideration –

JANE. Have you not seen the video?

LOYD. I was made aware of it but I wanted to get your permission before I –

>   (**JANE** *is scrolling on her phone, hands it to him.)*

Please don't feel pressured to show me –

JANE. Everybody I know has already seen it.

>   (*From the phone, the sound of a woman [**JANE**] screaming. She's in a crowded office.*

She screams and screams. We hear co-workers attempting to calm her down, the clicks of camera phones. The video ends. **LOYD** *looks at* **JANE**, *almost for the first time – the video has deeply affected him, something has shifted. He takes a moment to collect himself.* **JANE** *watches him. He hands her the phone back, at a loss.)*

LOYD. I'm so sorry...

  ...

JANE. I had a bad day.

But I'm doing *a lot* better now.

LOYD. Would getting let go from this job be the worst thing?

JANE. That would be the worst thing that could happen to me, yes, and so I'm just like...

I'm really scared.

LOYD. Scared of...?

JANE. Of you not being able to make the right decision.

LOYD. I'm only going to do what we both feel is best for you – I am a professional at the top of my field, I will –

JANE. But it's the field that's the problem.

Because people with your job come into work so desperate to connect trauma A to trauma D so they always do – it's a self-fulfilling prophecy or whatever. They hear that my mom and my best friend are both "EMOTIONALLY DISTANT" and they go "SEEEE?" – and like that way of thinking feels so emblematic of how we're supposed to look at the world nowadays where it's like "poverty is because of racism in housing which is because of capitalism" and at a certain point you're just saying everything is fucked and everyone's abused and when everything's connected it feels like nothing's connected. That way of thinking fully rots your brain – you stop being able to see what's right in front of your face, you stop being able to talk to people. It's endless and hopeless because you just get trapped in the like "discourse" of it all and you just end up mindlessly reposting GoFundMes all day, begging for spare change on your little Instagram street corner on behalf of strangers instead of actually doing something so I'm just not sure therapy aligns with how I deal with things.

LOYD. I think that's a brave perspective to own – that a popular mode of thought doesn't align with how you as the individual actually see things.

JANE. I don't own it though. I'd never put that out there. I'd get ripped apart.

LOYD. Ripped apart by who?

JANE. On like Twitter or Instagram. Like people I went to college with would explode at me.

LOYD. Even though you're just expressing your own personal opinion?

JANE. Yes?

LOYD. Do you think people care that much about what you post on the internet?

JANE. I don't want to give anyone another weapon to use against me.

LOYD. Who would want to use a weapon against you?

JANE. People.

LOYD. And are these people the reason you carry a gun?

JANE. No.

LOYD. And so why do you carry it?

JANE. I just carry it on days where I feel like I should.

LOYD. What comes to mind when you think about those days?

JANE. Uhm... I don't know.

Days where I feel bad?

LOYD. And, for you, how does feeling bad feel?

JANE. Uhm yeah it's just like... like it's just like those days where you wish you could just BE in the hospital.

You know? / That doesn't make sense out loud.

LOYD. Would you want to tell me more about that?

JANE. Uhm...sure – I don't mean days where I want to hurt myself.

I haven't ever done that in any sort of serious way ever. Like not in any way where the end result was like "I want to be dead" or even like "I hate myself."

LOYD. But you've engaged in self-harm / in the past?

JANE. Yeah but in like teenager ways like – this is different than that.

LOYD. You had just said you didn't feel like hurting yourself –

JANE. I don't.

LOYD. Gotcha, OK, and so when you say you want to go to the hospital...?

JANE. I realize this doesn't make a lot of sense –

LOYD. You're being very clear-headed and articulate buuttt I'm not sure I quite grasp the – is it that you're wanting to be cared for, to be –

JANE. I just want to lie down.

LOYD. Be my guest / if you –

JANE. No like at the hospital...they just force you to sit still.

LOYD. I see, so it's moreso being overwhelmed – maybe in your job, your day-to-day – you feel –

JANE. Today for example.

Today I woke up and it took me a long time to tell if I was still dreaming.

This happens to me most mornings – it's like I don't fit inside my body so I have to lie there and jam myself into my skin by forcing myself to remember like "OK I'm HERE, this is happening, it's genuinely Tuesday" – but then as soon as I'm fully awake I start to panic – it's a panic I'm so used to at this point that it's almost comforting.

It's like there's another person there with me, rubbing my back, telling me to keep going as I march into the bathroom and I brush my teeth and fuck around with my hair and eat my muesli and I drink my coffee and as I do each of those things the panic turns them into little missions – I have to NAIL flossing, I have to DESTROY my emails from Nordstrom Rack. I delete them and I EMPTY the trash and I imagine my emails burning. These little morning routine fucking inconsequential things become a sense of real...purpose...but on days like today there just isn't anything else – there's only me and the panic, alone together.

And so that's when I carry the gun.

It felt so obvious – riding the bus here with all of these strangers – I needed to feel it against my chest.

But honestly on days like today I just wish I could be in the ER where there are no choices at all.

LOYD. Should we go down the street to Saint Francis Memorial?

JANE. It's not about actually literally going.

LOYD. Going to the hospital after your incident – was that a positive / experience –

JANE. I wasn't super lucid when I was there but like in theory, being there would be nice because when you're in the hospital you don't have to "make sense" and you can just lie there while everyone replies to your Instagram story of you in the gown with the scary machines. Everyone stops to ask – they take the time to ask how you are in a way that's actually asking. In the real world nobody gives you their time and so what GOOD are friends and family – all of these people who allegedly love me – what is their VALUE if nobody has time for me?

…

And in this fantasy I'd have these deep, meaningful relationships with the nurses.

LOYD. Meaningful in what sense?

JANE. I'd remind them why they chose to be nurses in the first place.

And them working so hard would motivate me to get better.

And there'd be this like racial element that people don't like to admit is there but I feel like it's a thing for people like me, like white "liberal" people, where it's this safe space to get to know a person of color, like one of the Black or Latinx nurses, in this way where – or Asian nurses too – in this way where there's distance but you still get to feel like you CONNECTED, like you extended a hand across the aisle or whatever and made a friend with someone you wouldn't normally talk to. And obviously it's not real because they have to be nice to you and you're not your full like deeply subconsciously racist self but for a moment you live in this American fantasy where you can connect with any and everyone and being white doesn't matter. And all of that feels good.

…

Was any of that helpful?

You only wrote a few words down.

LOYD. I was listening.

JANE. You just wrote like "no chance" and "fucking crazy"?

LOYD. Just noting points to return to –

JANE. Awesome, let's return to whichever.

LOYD. Do you really think you're a racist?

JANE. What – no. No. I mean yes. That's not the point, of course I'm racist. Everyone's racist. I'm not even trying to be controversial, I think we'd be better off if we all admitted it.

LOYD. Do you feel like you can't connect with people?

JANE. I think everyone feels that way.

LOYD. Can you tell me a bit more about that?

JANE. It's just like I said – everyone's racist and we're all alone.

That's sort of our brand in 2020 as humans.

LOYD. How long have you been feeling this panic?

JANE. The panic did indeed start around when I started my job.

I know, I get it, but it's an unfortunate, manageable symptom of doing something important.

LOYD. So...part of you wants to be in the hospital...but you don't want to be in therapy – / hey now –

    (**JANE** *reaches into her tote.*)

Hey hey HEY HEY –

    (**JANE** *pulls out a tin of Altoids.**)

---

* A license to produce *JOB* does not include a license to publicly display any branded logos or trademarked images. Licensees must acquire rights for any logos and/or images or create their own.

JANE. WHAT? WHAT? – Oh.

...

Oh my god.

(Laughs, despite herself.)

I'm so sorry – wait what the fuck, you must have just had a heart attack.

LOYD. ...

You're keeping me on my toes.

JANE. OK well now you have to take one or it will all have been for nothing.

*(**LOYD** takes an Altoid, hesitates.)*

*(**JANE** eats one, showing him they're safe.)*

LOYD. *(Eats his Altoid.)* I'm curious – how has working where you work, working at G–

JANE. *(Fire alarm.)* Don't say the – sorry. Just if you could please not.

LOYD. You don't want me to say the name of your employer?

JANE. I still have a company phone.

LOYD. You're concerned they're listening in – hey I wouldn't be shocked.

CNN will report about Chinese surveillance but is our Great Nation all that different?

JANE. Well I mean...my company is allowed to – it's in our start paperwork.

LOYD. Ah but you see that's how they become so big and powerful – that pesky fine print.

JANE. I'm not sure either of us is smart enough to know how a company like mine succeeds.

LOYD. I'm certain I'm not. Not so sure about you though.

JANE. Why do you think I'm smart?

LOYD. From what little I know about you, you moved out to the Bay from – was it Michigan?

JANE. Wisconsin.

LOYD. You moved out here all on your own, managed to snag a job at a big deal place –

JANE. Lots of people do that though...

LOYD. I think you know you're smart.

JANE. Being smart's overrated.

I'd rather be hot honestly.

LOYD. Do you think of yourself as unattractive?

JANE. If I look too good nobody at work will take me seriously so I hope I'm like a 6? 6.5? I lived in LA for a few years after school and that made me feel fully hideous.

LOYD. SoCal's a real double-edged sword – nasty people, gorgeous weather.

JANE. Really? I sort of loved the people there.

Like I didn't love them – they sucked – but they sucked in such an obvious way that it made everything easier – it was easy to know who to trust.

And I *hated* the weather, no fucking thank you.

The sun fully gaslights you in LA – whenever I felt depressed there was the sun being like "why are you sad??? It's seventy degrees out!"

LOYD. But you moved up here specifically for the job?

Specifically to work in "user support"?

JANE. User care, it – yeah almost two years ago now.

LOYD. Did you grow up interested in working with technology? Computers?

JANE. Uhm… I mean my parents were pretty lax – they didn't care about grades or anything so I guess yeah I didn't really grow up with like…career aspirations.

LOYD. What do they do for work?

JANE. My mom teaches anthro at the University of Wisconsin.

And my dad's an artist – he makes these abstract glass sculpture-type-things.

LOYD. That's awesome! Now that is really cool.

JANE. Is it?

LOYD. I'm getting into some crafty work myself so perhaps it's just cool to me.

JANE. What sort of crafts?

LOYD. Necklaces, little doodads –

> (*The sound of a car bomb.* **LOYD** *doesn't acknowledge it.* **JANE** *hears it but tries not to react.*)

– nothing near as professional as your father.

JANE. I'd love to see some of your stuff.

LOYD. I'll bring in some pictures next time.

JANE. Next time just keeps getting better and better.

> (**JANE** *moves her chair to block the door. Her mind is racing. Beat.* **LOYD** *weighs his options.*)

LOYD. Are you an only child?

JANE. Just me, yeah.

LOYD. So all the attention in the house was on you –

JANE. Two houses – my parents aren't together.

And you're not married.

LOYD. Sorry?

JANE. No wedding ring.

LOYD. I'm separated so yes I know firsthand how difficult it can be for a family –

JANE. Divorce was good for my parents.

LOYD. How so?

JANE. My mom cheated on my dad.

LOYD. That must have been hard for you.

JANE. I turned out alright but wait sorry if it helps – there's no history of mental illness in my family.

I assume that's why you were asking about my parents?

LOYD. You brought up your parents.

But we can chat about whatever you want.

JANE. I'll talk about anything that you feel will give you grounds to reinstate me.

LOYD. I don't want you to feel that I'm dictating the terms of the conversation.

JANE. I just don't want us to waste time.

LOYD. I'm interested in what *you* want to share.

JANE. But again, it's not really about what I want.

LOYD. Again, that's not true from my perspective.

JANE. I'm fine to talk about parents or divorce or whatever.

LOYD. Were you angry at your mother at all?

JANE. I was mostly pissed at my dad.

LOYD. What about his role in the divorce made you angry?

JANE. My dad's just such a "nice guy."

LOYD. And that, for you, is a bad thing?

JANE. Well yeah because nobody is "good" or "nice" – that's something you should have to earn every single day. But for my dad, the bar is so low for men his age – his whole life people have told him he's *sensitive* and therefore *exceptional, different* – "not like other men."

And my dad believes it because he's arrogant – he thinks being quiet makes him better than everyone else.

And so he never lets himself get angry – he's never yelled at me, even when I broke one of his pieces.

LOYD. A lot of men of his generation didn't have healthy models for conflict –

JANE. No he had a great childhood – nobody fucked him up, he doesn't have an excuse.

Honestly I just wish I actually knew him.

Instead I know a failed artist who mopes around silently demanding praise for courageously not watching the Super Bowl.

So after thirty years? Shit, I'd cheat on a guy like that.

LOYD. Have you told him that you're angry?

JANE. There'd be no point, he would just sulk and feel bad that he made me feel bad.

LOYD. Well but he's your parent – I'm sure he'd want to know how you're feeling.

JANE. Mostly when I talk to either of them now it's just convincing them I'm not going to jump off the Golden Gate Bridge.

LOYD. That's sort of a role reversal – you're attending to their perceived needs.

Do you feel like they gave you the attention *you* needed from *them*?

JANE. It was a perfectly nice granola middle class existence – nothing to cry about.

LOYD. Being sent to therapy so young, did that feel like them slapping a Band-Aid on the situation? What you needed was your parents' attention, what you got was a therapist?

Maybe that's why you don't love therapy?

JANE. Do you have kids?

LOYD. I do.

> *(The sound of a buzz saw.* **LOYD** *doesn't acknowledge it.* **JANE** *tries not to.)*

JANE. How old?

LOYD. *(Remembering.)* My son is...oh jeez.

He's twelve –

> *(The sound of a buzz saw.* **JANE** *shakes her head, willing the sound away. It stops.)*

Twelve going on twenty-five – he knows so much it's scary.

JANE. Like what?

LOYD. The other day he accused me of "gaslighting" him about his NBA 2K video game or something of the like and I just sat back and thought to myself "man oh man, where is this kid learning what that word even is?"

JANE. I mean it's the internet probably, right?

He's just trying to make sense of the world around him.

LOYD. I try to keep him off, but I don't know what he gets into at his mom's house.

JANE. Are you one of those parents who doesn't believe in screens?

LOYD. Welllll…the fact is I treat a lot of folks – especially the folks working in tech like yourself – who have folded a lot of self-worth into their phones –

JANE. *(Taking this personally.)* Sure but like before phones people tied their self-worth to sex or music or like – like the phone just has all those things in one place.

LOYD. I see a lot of people where the phone ends up exacerbating problems they're already experiencing – paranoia, insomnia, low self-esteem.

JANE. Ugh no TOTALLY – why are the young people *always* on their phones, accessing the greatest collection of art and knowledge in human history?

And plus it's like being on my phone as opposed to what?

LOYD. I hear what / you're saying but –

JANE. I was on BART the other day, headphones in, scrolling around, living my life, and this old man motions for me to pull my earbud out and he's like "hey beautiful. Enjoy the company of the people around you!"

So I'm supposed to keep off my phone to engage with creepy old strangers like…?

Get hit on or read yogurt ads – those are the two activities available to me on public transit.

LOYD. Sounds like a misguided attempt at being friendly – generational miscommunication or –

JANE. Right yes – a lot of men of his generation didn't have healthy models for…hitting on people? Being creepy?

LOYD. You don't think your phone has contributed to why you're here today?

JANE. The *phone* is never the problem – people do bad things, not phones.

All these apps, Twitter or whatever – they don't invent any new emotions.

If reading one tweet makes you harass a stranger then you were already a piece of shit.

It's people who dox and SWAT – not companies, not devices.

People focus on the bad stuff with phones because they're afraid – "ah it's new, ah it's different" – and so they tell young women – the ones who're best at phones – they tell us we're stupid because they're afraid of us – afraid of our potential, our sexuality, everything.

When a girl's on her phone she's "VAIN," she's "self-obsessed" and it's like "no dude, she has a fucking wilderness skill."

I *like* my phone – it's not an "addiction," I'm not "anti-social," it just truly makes me happy.

My mom chugs prosecco from Costco every night – we're all just coping, right?

And like – AH it's so fucking crazy – like *WHY* are Boomers so upset about us USING technology when they're the ones getting rich off of it?

Go buy some Snapchat stock, my guy – like if you truly think it's such an epidemic.

But no instead of being happy with having all the money, ALL the power – Boomers spend their time being mad that sixteen-year-old girls are using filters on Instagram to feel prettier.

Like why're you offended that we feel insecure?

We're protecting ourselves from the thoughts your shampoo commercials made us think!

Fucking Facetune is empowering – we're taking our own faces back!

Truly gimme something else, old dudes – if you're so PISSED I'm on my phone at night after doing random, meaningless shit all day on the planet you ruined.

Invent something better than a phone, I will probably buy it.

Like why are you so *terrified* of progress?

LOYD. You're asking me?

JANE. You hate tech, right?

LOYD. I have a computer and a cell phone but I'm not much of an "app" user per se.

JANE. Tech's obviously ruined a lot of what brought people like you out here.

LOYD. People like me?

JANE. Your office has sort of a hippie Haight-Ashbury thing going on.

LOYD. I'm personally more concerned with what tech seems to do to people than the latent effect it has on places.

JANE. You don't care about gentrification?

People getting priced out – losing their houses?

LOYD. Do you care that you might be complicit in that sort of thing?

JANE. For someone to move in, someone has to have already been evicted.

It's the hippies who wrote the strict housing laws to make it so nobody can build low-income apartments next to their cutesy rowhouses.

JANE. You scapegoat us – the "transplants," the people moving here to build new ways to communicate and learn – you villainize us because tech bros and hippies are at war.

And we are winning.

LOYD. Well historically our kind is not the best at fighting wars.

I might posit that that spirit of rebellion, that questioning of power structures, may well have *given way* to Silicon Valley.

Perhaps both "cultures" are centered on pleasure – an immediate, self-involved pleasure.

Perhaps we've traded psychedelics for a slow drip of dopamine that comes from these devices in our pockets, the difference being we've gone from exploring our own minds to having our minds harvested for market research.

JANE. Well like...that's not that original of a thought.

LOYD. Well it has that in common with most thoughts.

JANE. Hippies were white kids from the suburbs who came out here to take drugs and fuck with impunity and now they're pissed something productive is replacing their fifty-year-long drum circle.

LOYD. But let's look at history.

The legacy of "hippiedom" – the end of the draft, the women's movement –

JANE. The legacy of the 60s is an obsession with aesthetics.

To be anti-war you had to wear a tie-dye shirt and grow your hair out and so now, today, I'm not allowed to have "good politics" and wear Lululemon.

Literally all I can remember about the first semester of college was trying to figure out how to dress like I cared about social justice and the cafeteria workers' union and gender-neutral bathrooms. To give a shit I had to smell like shit – I had to wear ratty t-shirts to be publicly accepted as a good person.

LOYD. Did you enjoy college?

JANE. Loved it.

Did you?

LOYD. A great deal.

I'm glad to hear it's still a good time.

JANE. Where did you go to school?

LOYD. Just over the bridge.

JANE. Berkeley?

LOYD. That's the one.

> (*A car motor starts. It continues under the scene, the engine revving. A crowd hoots and hollers.* **JANE** *is perturbed.*)

JANE. Is that where you met your ex-wife?

LOYD. In a sense but actually –

JANE. Is she younger than you?

LOYD. Why do you ask?

JANE. Your son is young and you're...yeah, you're like old to have a twelve-year-old son.

LOYD. She was a graduate student of mine and we reconnected long after we'd both left –

JANE. Do you mind that I'm asking you questions?

LOYD. It's not how I usually do things.

JANE. So you want me to stop.

> *(The car sounds begin to fade.)*

LOYD. I want to hear about college.

What were your friends like?

JANE. They were cringey rich assholes.

LOYD. And these were your friends?

JANE. They were sort of just fascinated by me.

They all thought being from the Midwest was exotic almost.

LOYD. So did you...enjoy being friends with them?

JANE. It was fun – I partied too much.

They all talked about BIG things they were going to do – join the PeaceCorps in Benin, open a DIY venue in Detroit.

They would snort Ketamine and post like "REQUIRED READING FOR ANYONE WHO WAS RAISED BY A JAMAICAN NANNY" and then it'd be an article called like "How The CIA Appropriated Reggae Music To Train The KKK" or some made-up nonsense.

They were allowed to be anyone, they could do anything, they didn't even have to be gay to shout about how "queer" they were.

I tricked myself into being like "OK I like drugs, I make out with girls at parties, I'm just like these people."

LOYD. College is a lonely time for a lot of people.

> *(**JANE** doesn't respond.)*

The "queer" thing – that terminology took me awhile to grasp.

Because when I was a kid "queer" was almost a slur.

JANE. I'm aware, yes.

LOYD. That took me awhile to learn.

JANE. How do you learn something like that?

LOYD. Sorry?

JANE. How do you learn new things? At your age.

LOYD. My daughter explained / it to me –

JANE. You have a son and a daughter?

LOYD. I have a son and a daughter.

(Click.)

(**LOYD** *paces around the room – a soldier.)*

(In Russian.) Prokommentiruyte chto vy khotite chtoby ya s nim sdelal. Khotite chtoby ya snova yego szheg?

(Click.)

(**LOYD** *is a teenager.**)

Daaaammn Daniel... damn Daniel.... DAMN Daniel, back at it AGAIN with the white vans!

(Click.)

(**LOYD** *is back in his chair. He's young, frustrated, filled with a simmering rage.)*

I'm twenty-two years old and I'm still a virgin. I've never even kissed a girl. I've been through college for two and a half years, more than that actually, and I'm still a virgin.

(Click.)

---

* Any recognizable meme/internet thing will do here. In our original production this was a certain famous men's body wash commercial.

(We're back in the room.)

LOYD. Where did you go?

JANE. What?

LOYD. Just now, where did you go?

You sort of...went somewhere else for a moment.

JANE. Your daughter, is she –

*(A knock at the door. **JANE** doesn't move.)*

(Beat. What happens now?)

*(Another knock. **JANE** jumps.)*

LOYD. *(To the person in the hall.)* Just a second.

*(Back to **JANE**.)* That's my next appointment.

JANE. I don't feel like we're done.

Right?

*(**LOYD** fumbles with his words.)*

You have to finish your report.

LOYD. OK.

I'm going to need to text them.

JANE. And say what?

LOYD. I'm going to cancel our appointment.

I'm going to go to my desk and get my phone –

JANE. I'm not like...imposing anything but –

LOYD. Sure.

JANE. I need us to do this today but if you...well what do
you think we should do?

LOYD. I'm going to text them, I don't want them to walk
in and –

JANE. That would be insane – to just barge into somebody / else's session?

LOYD. May I text them?

JANE. You don't have to ask permission just – yeah, text away.

> (**LOYD** *texts.*)

And then just please show me what you said.

> (**LOYD** *slyly deletes something, types.*)
>
> (*Shows* **JANE** *his phone.*)
>
> (**JANE** *reads.*)
>
> (*Presses send for him, gives a little thumbs up.*)

LOYD. You can go if you want – I should be able to finish your evaluation.

JANE. You've barely asked me anything.

LOYD. I think I have what I need.

JANE. What do you "have"?

LOYD. I have what we've discussed –

JANE. So I can go back?

LOYD. I need to sit down and review my notes.

Alone.

JANE. I know I haven't done my best –

LOYD. How long are you going to keep us here?

JANE. Just please let me show you I am ready – I've *been* ready for months.

LOYD. If you're ready to go back to a job that triggered your public breakdown, you can show me by letting / us both –

JANE. Is that what they told you?

That all this happened because of my work?

LOYD. It's fairly obvious based on / how you –

JANE. No no no – it was Syd's fault.

(**LOYD** *is visibly confused.*)

JANE. Sorry he – Syd's this guy who I had this shitty thing with in college.

He got me pregnant in college.

LOYD. And why was your breakdown his fault?

JANE. Because he's the worst.

LOYD. What about him makes him the worst?

JANE. He like fully hates himself and at the same time he's judging everyone all the time.

He hates parties, hates talking to people – like just a deeply embarrassing person.

Shorter than me...

LOYD. Sounds reminiscent of the traits you really don't like in your father.

JANE. Right that's like an all-time like therapy classic, that's really perceptive.

I don't have a kid by the way – I had an abortion.

LOYD. I'm sorry you had to go through that –

JANE. You're making the same face everyone makes.

LOYD. I apologize if –

JANE. The face is almost apologetic. But it's also very TENSE.

'Cause you're like a Berkeley dad so you know you're supposed to support my rights.

But somewhere deep down there's a part of you that thinks I'm a slutty kid who doesn't know how condoms work and that maybe makes you feel like a bad guy.

LOYD. That's not how I'm feeling but I value your perspective.

> (**JANE** *shrugs.*)

Well thank you for sharing that with me.

I know some women prefer to keep their history with abortion very quiet.

That must have been a challenging time.

JANE. I can handle challenge.

LOYD. I don't see you as someone who loves being challenged per se –

JANE. What kind of person are you?

> (*The sounds of pornography.*)

LOYD. In what sense?

JANE. Can you handle being challenged?

LOYD. I am someone who thrives on being challenged – I can say that with some confidence.

Today perhaps serving as some evidence of that.

JANE. Where do you live?

> (*Someone spits on someone else.*)

LOYD. Sorry?

JANE. What's your address?

Where do you sleep every night?

> (*An orgasm.*)

LOYD. That's less of a "challenge" and more of a piece of private information –

JANE. How am I doing on my review – like out of ten?

LOYD. I –

JANE. You're safe – stop looking at me like that.

Please be better, you can't be afraid of me –

LOYD. I'm not afraid of you –

JANE. Maybe you should be.

LOYD. I'm not trying to insult you, I'm not trying to-to-to *deceive* you – this is about *me* getting to know you –

JANE. Do you feel like you know me?

LOYD. I know you better than I did thirty minutes ago but –

JANE. Do you like me?

LOYD. Do you want me to like you?

JANE. You can just say no.

LOYD. No no of course I like you –

JANE. What reason have I given you to like me?

LOYD. You see the world in a unique way.

I enjoy people like that.

JANE. I don't want you to like me – I want you to understand me.

LOYD. If I understood you, don't you think I'd like you?

JANE. Do you think you're good at your job?

LOYD. I do, yes.

JANE. You've been a therapist for a long time – forty years in this office.

LOYD. Forty years in the practice, yes.

The office is actually somewhat new – about ten years old but...I take it you looked me up online?

JANE. There weren't any pictures of you.

Do you think you're still in your prime?

Like do you think you're as good as you ever were?

LOYD. These past few years have been the most rewarding of my career, which I think in turn makes me better at my job.

For instance it's clear to me that Syd is someone you have complicated feelings about –

JANE. Syd's just Syd, I don't know.

LOYD. What don't you know?

JANE. I mean sure all through college we saw each other every night – we had sex every night.

But then obviously when I needed something, if I was feeling stressed or whatever, he would pull back and become my "FRIEND."

He would make that very clear – he'd call me bro, dude, homie, ask me if I thought other guys were attractive.

...

I didn't tell him about the pregnancy, not at the time.

I knew he'd make it this traumatic thing HE was having to endure.

LOYD. Did you ever consider carrying the pregnancy to term?

JANE. Not for a single second but...yeah. No.

And like...my college friends who I told, they talked about it like it was this no-brainer thing. They made it sound "easy" or like...*fun* – it felt like they were excited for me to get the abortion.

Going to the clinic, past the bullshit loser protestors, that wasn't like...girl boss Roe v Wade Hilary Clinton yes mama like – and not that my friends were even like that, they were literally all socialists but like...yeah.

JANE. And you're not supposed to think about it like this but like... I felt close to Syd and I couldn't... I couldn't get rid of this feeling that came from bringing a little life into the – even though I *know* a fetus isn't – whatever, yeah.

LOYD. Do you still feel connected to him?

JANE. I don't feel connected to anyone from that time in my life.

LOYD. Not your friends?

JANE. Especially not them.

LOYD. What do you think is at the root of that?

JANE. After school I lived in my friend Zoe's guesthouse in LA.

Her dad was a life coach and her mom was like an oil heiress or something.

All we did was do coke, gossip about people from college, and eat at Michelin-starred taco trucks – it was what a twelve-year-old thinks being sixteen will be like.

But one day it just sort of hit me – I was nothing like them.

I didn't have an uncle who could get me a job on a TV show.

So now I help people – my college friends talk about how people need help.

Any idiot can canvass for Bernie, but if they actually wanted to do something – like to the degree they claimed – they'd kill their parents and redistribute the inheritance.

LOYD. That feels less sustainable from where I'm sitting but...I'd love to hear how you help people.

JANE. I make sacrifices.

LOYD. Why does helping involve a sacrifice?

JANE. That's just how it works, it's a transference of energy, you have to take the bad out of the world and store it in your body. It's not about giving something – "donating" your money or your time – no, it's about being willing to extract the darkness and take it with you, fucking carry it around with you every day.

LOYD. Carry it with you like your gun?

JANE. If that's what you want it to mean, go off. Sure.

LOYD. I'm just trying to understand.

JANE. I can't tell how hard you're trying.

LOYD. I've been trying very hard, I have been quite generous in fact –

JANE. This is your job.

LOYD. It's OK if you feel hurt – by Syd, by your parents, by feeling like you need to be here –

JANE. Most people go their entire lives without knowing what they were put on Earth to do and I have that so no – I'm not "hurt."

I'm lucky.

LOYD. I don't think anybody on Earth would care if you came out and said "I am having a hard time." You aren't helping anyone by denying your / own –

JANE. I'm not denying anything – I feel it all – and it's a privilege to suffer as much as I do.

LOYD. Can you see how that is a deeply concerning thing to hear?

JANE. I didn't ask anyone to be concerned – if it were up to me I'd be at work.

LOYD. You do want people to be concerned – that's your hospital fantasy.

JANE. Why do you think all this shit has happened to me?

LOYD. How do you mean?

JANE. Like why do you think I'm like this?

Diagnose me with something.

LOYD. It takes more than one meeting to properly –

JANE. I don't think we're the right match.

Because if we were you'd see there's nothing "wrong" with me.

LOYD. And I've said, I don't believe in the dichotomy of right and wrong when it comes to –

JANE. You're wasting your time.

LOYD. Here with you?

JANE. Doing what you do because it's like… like why is it always about the person on the couch with you guys?

Why not treat the problem at the source?

Why don't you get out of the chair and fight for the people who need you?

It's things outside this room that make your patients paranoid and depressed.

LOYD. Did you just diagnose yourself?

JANE. Yeah totally, you nailed it.

LOYD. If I may – my only goal is to help you.

JANE. You're ASSUMING I need help!

LOYD. This is all very hard for me.

…

I am really struggling here.

JANE. So you're giving up?

LOYD. I do wonder what would happen – crazy idea here – if you stopped attacking me and listened a bit.

Because honestly my dear, I'm not sure what methods you seem so sure that you've acquired, what justifications you have for feeling like you don't need my help but clearly your way isn't working.

You're buying street Xanax from Mexico.

You are lying to yourself and-and-and I mean, I mean I am hesitant to say any of this to you after what you've put us through –

JANE. I made a mistake –

LOYD. You're mad at your father for playing the victim but I think you do a bit of that yourself – nothing ever seems to be your fault.

You have to form a binary opinion of everyone and everything because you're desperate for any semblance of control.

I think on your best days you're an extremely competent person but where you falter is your unwillingness to accept the idea that someone might actually understand you.

You don't know yourself and so you can't accept the idea that anyone else might.

(*JANE is hurt, unsure how to respond.*)

You're not behaving like someone who wants to impress me so she can get her job back.

Frankly I don't think you want to go back there – you're afraid to utter the company's name.

You want me to protect you from having to return to this job.

I mean GOD, what kind of person would I be if I *let* you go back in the state you're in?

JANE. Let's finish the session –

LOYD. THERE IS NO SESSION!

From the moment you pulled out the gun there was no – this is not what I do!

Please realize what is happening here.

You are holding me hostage.

Your finger could have slipped and my son wouldn't have a dad.

JANE. My finger wouldn't *slip*, I'm not –

LOYD. I lost my daughter when she was thirteen years old.

My daughter took her own life when she was thirteen years old.

>   *(Beat.)*

>   (**JANE** *is frozen.*)

My daughter would have these episodes when she was little.

She would cry and cry and cry.

It was almost violent – it was excruciating as a parent.

Someone so small carrying that kind of pain...

Nothing we did would make it stop – she would cry until she passed out.

Watching that video...I missed that part of her...for the first time, I missed her rage.

...

But what got me out of bed after my daughter passed, was knowing that I had a chance to help save the next one.

I knew I wouldn't give up on that next person – *could not* even.

And that's why now, professionally, I seek out people like you.

I tell colleagues – I tell them "send me the ones you think are hopeless, the ones you think are beyond help."

I am the best at what I do, I can make a difference for you.

I'd like to have us both leave here today feeling like we moved in some kind of right direction or that we established enough trust where you'll follow through on a referral.

Because I can say from experience – how we process the world is so much more important than what actually happens to us.

...

But the first step is both of us leaving this office –

JANE. I remind you of your daughter?

> (**JANE**'s *heart is beating out of her chest. The lights quietly get brighter, hotter. The sounds of...everything. The whole world. Horrors unimaginable.*)
>
> (*She's having a panic attack. She's resisting the idea that it's happening. She's silent. She shuts her eyes. She paces, bounces up and down. She might even leave the stage and come back. She is outside of the play.*)
>
> (**LOYD** *takes out and dons a mask – it almost looks like him...but a deformed version, a monster version. He picks up the tote bag with the gun in it.*)

LOYD. Are you alright?

> (*Blackout.*)

(Beat.)

(Lights up. We're back in the room.)

*(**JANE** is mid-panic, not moving. **LOYD** looks at her, trying to decide what to do next.)*

(This lasts as long as it needs to.)

LOYD. A few deep breaths.

JANE. I'm not a BREATHER really uh... I'm not a uh, I'm not...

LOYD. Deep breath in.

JANE. Stop, stop, stop –

LOYD. And out.

One more time. Deep breath in.

*(**JANE** deep breath in.)*

And out.

(And out.)

(Beat.)

LOYD. I think it's time for us to go.

JANE. I can't.

LOYD. I'm not going to send your company any kind of evaluation –

JANE. I'm not leaving.

LOYD. You had a panic attack, you're under a lot of stress, you –

*(**JANE** is getting emotional.)*

The door is right there.

*(**JANE** walks to the door. Beat. She turns.)*

JANE. If I give you the gun will you shoot yourself?

...

You must want to.

>   (**LOYD** *is not sure how to answer.*)

How do you not want to?

LOYD. I don't know what you want me to say here.

>   *(Silence.)*

JANE. Do you know what I do every day?

LOYD. User care.

JANE. Yes.

Or so at my company it's called User Care, but most places call it Content Moderation.

When I started it was three of us.

We have our own little building on the edge of campus.

My company invented these bots – these little computer programs – that travel all over the internet flagging things as illicit or inappropriate or obscene.

They do this because nobody wants to see their ads appear on a neo-Nazi website, right?

...

RIGHT?

LOYD. Right.

JANE. But the bots can't do everything – there are errors, toss-ups, mistakes that require someone to physically review the thing.

And that's what I do, that's who I am.

That first morning I sat down at my desktop – I had no idea what to expect.

JANE. Our algorithm fed me a video from the 90s – something that was circulating on Reddit and finding its way to other sites.

The video was from the civil war in Sierra Leone.

Government soldiers tied a rebel to two trucks.

He was a little boy, not older than thirteen.

The trucks drove in opposite directions and split the boy in half.

And I sat there watching like "fuck" you know like "FUCK" like "WHAT THE FUCK" but then...I realized I could flag the video – I could drag it into the big "X" folder.

I tried to search it – it was gone.

I buried it – nobody will ever have to see that video again.

And in that moment, for the first time since I could remember,

I felt like I had actually accomplished something.

But I never "enjoyed" my work.

Every day I resisted the urge to look away.

There were red rooms – someone being tortured live on webcam.

Horses fucking women, people fucking dead animals.

Car crash compilations, mass graves, heroin overdoses, a website for strep throat fetishists.

People eating glass, people sticking glass up their assholes and vaginas.

To be effective in my role I had to come into work fucking infuriated.

I had to actually reckon with what had happened to these people.

Before my job I didn't give a shit.

I couldn't do anything to help so I was afraid to care.

I'd scroll past the body of a Black person murdered by the police and all I would do is share that dead person's name on Twitter.

But now, because of my job I'm allowed to care.

And caring made me responsible.

I became an adult with a real life – I flew home without connecting through Denver, I bought plants, I got a scooter.

It's trendy to have everything be "inclusive" these days but it's only through anointing some people as special that any sort of progress happens.

My company is elitist, and everyone should thank God that it is.

It really felt like working at the center of the universe.

We have panko crusted tilapia every day – you can take a private yoga class, you can work from the Singapore office. It's easy to dismiss those perks as "adult daycare" or whatever but until you've worked there, you won't get it. It's considered like…"dystopian" to love your tech job but anyone who says that hasn't tasted the alkali waters I've tasted.

That's what bonds us – my co-workers – we are people unafraid to be important.

My co-workers are ambitious – they're shameless.

At first I was looking for the "cool kids" table, the group I should try to join.

But all I had to do was work as hard as everyone else and knowing exactly what you have to do?

That's freedom.

JANE. Everything was good – great even...and then... well you saw.

LOYD. That's a horrible thing to have to do every day.

It's not your fault / that –

JANE. I know it's not my fault.

LOYD. Right because this is not a job a person should have.

And you tried to suppress your feelings of panic and one day it all came to a head.

JANE. I didn't freak out because of my job.

...

Syd texted me.

He was in town for a conference or something – I hadn't seen him since graduation.

He asked if we could hang out.

I wanted to prove to myself that I wasn't that person anymore – I was over it.

I went to his hotel room.

At first he was the same – he talked at me about bike lanes for like twenty minutes.

We smoked and we were watching some weird anime thing and it...like it just slipped out.

I told him about the pregnancy.

I was so high I like gestured, like physically tried to stuff the words back into my mouth.

He didn't say anything at first and I was like "yep, knew it."

It was his wet dream basically – a woman caring enough to keep a secret from him, but...he...he cried.

...

And he hugged me.

And he told me he was sorry that I had to go through that alone.

He told me he loved me.

I asked if he meant as a friend or as just like a person or...he said he wasn't sure.

He said that he was never sure, which I knew but to hear him actually *say* it... we just sat there.

Eventually we muttered goodbye and I left.

Walking out of his hotel...I felt so fucking young.

Like I was too young to be out on the street by myself.

...

The next day I had to present to our managers on how the new bots were doing.

I walked into one of the main buildings, went to the fourth floor.

The elevator dinged and all of a sudden I was standing on a desk, looking down at all these faces – people looking up at me, horrified.

I heard someone screaming.

I look around to see who it was and realized it was me.

I stood there in the middle of the office and I screamed.

I saw people's phones, I saw the security guards rush in.

I remember thinking like "why is nobody helping me?"

"Why can't everyone see I need help?"

I tried to make eye contact with them – my co-workers – trying to prove to them that I was one of them, that I deserved that help.

JANE. My throat felt raw, like there was a scraped knee stuck to the roof of my mouth.

They sent me to the emergency room.

They put me under – not sure for how long.

When I woke up, the videos were everywhere.

I had achieved the new American dream – I had gone viral.

"TECH EMPLOYEE FREAKS OUT AND WE CAN'T STOP WATCHING."

I was everywhere on Earth, screaming like a crazy person – BEING a crazy person.

I was a meme.

I was "when you ask to speak to the manager but the person behind the counter is the manager."

I was mental health.

I was a loud cunt.

I was "that feel when it's Monday."

I was a typical white woman.

I was everything wrong with tech.

I was how everyone feels thinking about the election.

I can't do anything in real life anymore.

When I try to go outside I get recognized.

People sneak pictures of me in line at Walgreens.

Today, on my way here, a man asked if he could record me saying happy birthday to his friend.

I'm famous and nobody knows who I am.

That first week my parents came out and stayed with me.

They didn't let me go to the bathroom alone – I could barely move without them flinching.

My college friends wrote long, elaborate Instagram posts about how much they "loved me."

I was just clout to them now – I knew they were telling everyone in Silver Lake that they knew the crazy girl from that video.

Obviously I never heard from Syd.

The company decided they needed to get behind me, that that was politically smarter.

I wouldn't accept any of their severance packages, they knew there were dozens of reporters in my inbox.

They fired everyone who leaked the video.

They put me on paid indefinite leave.

I emailed them every day – finally last week they agreed to let me back with a therapist's approval.

Because after all of that, all I wanted was a chance to go back.

LOYD. But you said it yourself – your job is about protecting advertisers.

JANE. The internet isn't some fringe "young people" thing anymore – it's where we live.

It's our home and I am the front line of defense – there's nobody else.

All of the worst things in the world come right to my computer screen.

I've had fifty-four different people in the chair next to me – the turnover was slowing us down.

A month or so before I was put on leave I convinced them we didn't need two people.

I negotiated a raise and now it's just me.

LOYD. Why should all this burden fall to you?

JANE. It's not a burden.

LOYD. What would you call it then?

JANE. Power.

For the first time in my life I have power.

Or had.

LOYD. By now I'm sure they've given your job to someone else.

JANE. They'll "burnout" soon – they always do.

Nobody else can do what I do.

LOYD. This is unskilled labor.

The job is just the willingness to be tortured.

You see that don't you?

In any other context this would be torture.

JANE. That doesn't change the fact that there's work to do.

I can't walk away from this.

As soon as my parents left I was completely alone.

I sat in my apartment and I imagined the people on their knees, waiting to die.

I imagined the women in the scat fetish videos, who eat shit to feed their families.

Without that release – destroying the videos, sealing them away – without that it was like my whole brain was in my spine, my whole brain was being stretched like it was going to break.

So I started searching anything I could remember from work, anything I could identify as being from the continental U.S.

I couldn't just wait around.

I went to the darkest corners, I gave my laptop every virus there is.

I learned how to look for different architectural styles, what motels used which rug patterns.

If I could find a face I could reverse search and then there they were – their LinkedIn, their Facebook.

These freaks are living among us – we sit next to them at movies, we cut them off in traffic.

LOYD. What would you do when you found these people?

JANE. I mean I'd send letters to their families, I tried to get them fired.

A couple times I went to their houses – I drove hundreds of miles.

I'd knock on their doors and then I'd watch them – the men from the videos – I'd watch them look stupid and confused on their front steps.

They were real.

Seeing them I imagined everything they didn't film, all the harm they'd caused.

But yeah I couldn't fucking do anything.

I wasn't strong enough to do anything.

…

But being here with you…it's not up to me anymore.

LOYD. What's not up to you?

> *(At some point in this speech she picks up the tote bag.)*

JANE. A few months ago, after I was put on leave, I found a guy who would make his children have sex.

…

Every week.

JANE. Sometimes he would scream at them, but most of the time he was "kind."

He would tell them how special they were, how well-behaved.

He knew them so well – he knew how to get them to listen.

He would be in the corner...watching.

He had different commands for what he wanted them to do – he would snap or clap or whistle.

They trusted him – he was their father.

You could see it in their eyes – they still thought he loved them.

They still wanted his love.

I found years and years of footage.

And he still has new videos popping up all the time – every Thursday he uploads.

I had never seen any of his videos at work – he was getting through the cracks.

All of these videos were unmonitored, unflagged – circulating.

He has "fans" – multiple websites, backup accounts.

He's methodical, organized.

People like him, they aren't sick – there's nothing "wrong" with them.

They're evil.

It's the evil every God warns about.

They come from nature.

You can't escape them – you have to defeat them.

I had to get back to work – I had to use our tech to stop his growth.

He didn't miss a week – every Thursday – STILL – he publishes a new one.

But my company wasn't responding to me.

I had to start on my own.

He didn't speak much but sometimes he shouted from the other room.

I watched every single clip hundreds of times.

I studied regional dialects – the little intonations in speech, the things we don't even realize are accents.

Hours and hours of tapes before I could conclude he was somewhere in Northern California.

He kept his face hidden – it's like he knew I was coming for him.

But I couldn't give up – I wasn't sleeping.

I pieced together fragments of his face – half an eye, the tip of an ear.

It took weeks, a lot of process of elimination.

Even with the rough collage of how he looked, it wasn't enough.

I saw the corner of a college degree on the wall – I looked at thousands online – and based on font and shading I determined it was a undergraduate degree from Berkeley.

He wore this very unique handmade looking jewelry – little doodads.

LOYD. *(Realizing.)* Jane –

JANE. He had two children – a boy and a girl.

But a few years ago the girl died.

She was thirteen – he liked to advertise their ages.

These people – the "fans" – replied they were heartbroken.

JANE. He made compilations of her "best work."

And even after that he kept making videos with his son.

His son...this little boy...

...

Sometimes after he's done, he tucks his son into bed.

He livestreams – he lets these people watch his son sleep.

...

So I bought a gun.

What else could I do?

He could be anyone – he could live in my building.

And now I'm looking at you – you're not pixels anymore.

And after meeting you – you're never going to stop.

You don't regret any of it.

Nobody else is going to stop you.

    (Silence.)

LOYD. We can put my son on the phone right now.

We can put my ex-wife on the phone right now –

JANE. I'm good at this.

LOYD. So why don't we do this – you give the police your story and they can investigate me –

JANE. You saw me on the desk – they won't take me seriously.

LOYD. Jane, let's leave this office, / let's –

JANE. *(Taking out the gun.)* THERE'S NOWHERE TO GO.

I SEE YOU EVERYWHERE!

THERE'S NOTHING LEFT.

LOYD. Please –

JANE. When I walked in I saw your face and my hand moved on its own.

It can't be a coincidence – I was supposed to find you.

What are the odds that I just *happen* to end up in a room with you, / YOU of all people –

LOYD. The odds are one in a billion.

Maybe this is your own self-fulfilling prophecy – you are desperate to connect A to D.

You are desperate to make sense of what's happened to you.

JANE. I've been sitting here hoping it wasn't you – PRAYING – stopping myself from seeing it.

If I could *connect* with you it would prove you're not him.

You revealed all of it and I kept lying to myself –

LOYD. Of course we've connected, Jane.

You came in and you realized you needed to talk to someone.

When was the last time you spoke to another person face to face?

JANE. I've studied you – stop / trying to –

LOYD. Let's both go home.

You don't deserve the – I mean the things this company has forced you to watch –

JANE. None of this is about me!

LOYD. I know the pressure of having a job that is also your reason to live – a job you don't feel like you chose.

We are both people saddled with a calling.

LOYD. Mine is to care for the young woman here in this room.

Not some cog in a corporate machine, not some viral video,

but a person who has earned the right to be taken seriously.

My entire career has led me to right here.

I was destined to be your doctor.

JANE. *(Aiming the gun at him, stance firm.)* I'm done trying to live in the fucking future.

There's no next time, no referrals, no right direction – I'm done, I –

LOYD. I will give you your job back.

...

I think it would help you.

I will write you the recommendation you need.

They trust me –

JANE. You're just talking –

LOYD. You can be someone with friends and a career – someone who exists in the real world.

You can go back to the company you love and the people you admire.

They gave you this chance today – let's prove them right.

*(**JANE** tries to stay tough, resolute.)*

You love your job because you help people – you save us from having to see what you see. You give the victims their dignity.

Think about all the other people who still need you out there – all the people nobody else is willing to look at.

Let's say you're right.

Is killing one guy worth giving up on everyone else?

There will always be new videos.

...

If you shoot me both of our lives end.

> (**JANE** *is taking deep breaths, trying not to shake.*)

Let's get you back to work.

> (**JANE** *and* **LOYD** *stand there, her gun not moving.*)
>
> (*Click.*)
>
> (*Reset. Nothing has changed.*)
>
> (*Click.*)
>
> (*Reset. Nothing has changed.*)
>
> (*Click.*)
>
> (*Reset. Nothing has changed.*)
>
> (*Click.*)
>
> (*Reset. Nothing has changed.*)
>
> (*There is nothing beyond this moment – there is no alternative, no future.*)
>
> (*Slowly, she begins to lower the gun.*)
>
> (**LOYD** *takes a step towards her.*)
>
> (*Blackout.*)

End of Play

Milton Keynes UK
Ingram Content Group UK Ltd.
UKHW020447060824
446584UK00010B/159